Magic Molly

The Witch's Kitten

HOLLY WEBB

Scholastic Children's Books
An imprint of Scholastic Ltd
Euston House, 24 Eversholt Street, London, NW1 1DB, UK
Registered office: Westfield Road, Southam, Warwickshire, CV47 0RA
SCHOLASTIC and associated logos are trademarks and/or
registered trademarks of Scholastic Inc.

First published in the UK as *Molly's Magic: The Witch's Kitten* by Scholastic Ltd, 2009
This edition published by Scholastic Ltd, 2018

ISBN 978 1407 19272 7

A CIP catalogue record for this book
is available from the British Library.

Printed by CPI Group (UK) Ltd, Croydon, CR0 4YY
Papers used by Scholastic Children's Books are made
from wood grown in sustainable forests.

1 3 5 7 9 10 8 6 4 2

www.scholastic.co.uk

www.holly-webb.com

For Alice, with love

Chapter One

Molly and Sparkle

Molly dashed across the yard, her school bag thudding against her side. "I'm just going to see Dad!"

"Don't be long, Molly! You need to change out of your school uniform!" Mum called.

"I'll just be a minute! I only want to see if anyone I know is in the waiting room," Molly promised, as she reached the surgery door.

"Me too! Me too!" her little sister

Kitty begged, but Mum took her into the house for juice instead.

Molly Smith was seven years old. She lived with her mum and dad and Kitty at Larkfield Farm, just on the edge of the town. It was a lovely place to live, with a huge field behind the house to play in, and, best of all, it was right across the farmyard from the vet's surgery!

Molly's mum and dad ran Larkfield Vets. Her dad, Sam, was the vet and her mum, Jo, was one of the veterinary nurses, but she only worked part-time now.

Molly pushed the door open. Her heart gave an excited little thump. This was her favourite moment of the day. She looked eagerly round as the door swung closed behind her. Larkfield Farm Vets was usually really busy, and Molly always felt like she was missing the most interesting animals while she was at school! Today the waiting room was quiet, with only a grumpy-looking dog, and one lady with a cat-basket.

Molly knew the lady – it was Sarah, who worked at the flower shop just down the road from the farm. Molly and Kitty and their mum would walk past her cottage when they were out exploring, and Sarah sometimes invited them in for a biscuit. Molly liked to go, because Sarah had three gorgeous cats, and they all loved Molly to stroke them – even though Sarah said they were normally shy. Molly adored cats. And dogs. And mice and gerbils and parrots – well, anything with fur or feathers, really. . .

"Hi Sarah!" Molly knelt down a little way from the basket to peer in. "Who've you brought today?" Then she looked up excitedly. "Hey, that's not Mickey! Or Freckles or Maisy. Have you got *another* cat?"

Sarah nodded and sighed. "Yes. This is Sparkle. I suppose he's mine. . ."

Molly sat up and looked at her. "You suppose he is?" She frowned. "I don't understand."

"Sparkle just turned up in my garden a couple of days ago. I saw him on my way home from work, and said hello to him. I just thought he must belong to one of the neighbours. Then he nipped in while I was letting Freckles out – you know how she hates using the cat flap."

Molly giggled. Freckles was a *very* fussy

cat. She hated coming to the vets too.

"Anyway, he had his nose in one of our cat food bowls before I'd even shut the door. He was starving, poor kitten. Now it looks like he's adopted me."

"He's gorgeous," Molly said admiringly, peeking back into the basket. "Is he all grey?"

"Not even a white hair," Sarah agreed. "Oh, he's a real beauty." She shook her head, and sighed again, even while she was smiling down at the grey kitten.

Molly didn't notice the sigh. She was too busy looking at Sparkle. It was a little hard to see him properly in the depths of the basket, but she could tell he was beautiful, and so tiny. He had big, round, sparkling green eyes, and soft silver-grey fur. His whiskers were long, shiny and black.

Molly gazed delightedly down at him. How could such a lovely little kitten be a stray? His real owner must be very upset. Molly shuddered at the thought. If he were hers and she'd lost him, she wouldn't know *what* to do.

Sparkle looked up at Molly hopefully, and opened his mouth, showing a bright pink tongue. He gave a sad little mew that Molly knew meant, "Please take me out of this horrible basket!"

Molly smiled. "It won't be much

longer," she promised him. "My dad will see you in a minute."

Just then, Molly's dad popped his head round the door of the consulting room, and grinned at her. "I heard that. I wondered when you'd arrive, Molly. You're right though, I've finished with Mr Davies and Alf, so Sarah can come on in."

He held the door open for a man carrying a tank with a large lizard in it. Molly stared curiously as he carried it past her, wondering what was wrong with Alf. He looked bored, but that was all she

could see, and she had a feeling lizards looked like that a lot of the time.

"Definitely try him on crickets," Molly's dad called after Mr Davies, and Molly shuddered. *Uuurgh*. She was desperate to have a pet of her own, but she definitely didn't want anything she had to feed on live creepy-crawlies.

Sarah picked up Sparkle's basket, and Molly hopefully sneaked into the consulting room behind her. She'd told Mum she'd be back in a minute, but she really wouldn't be very long, and she *was* a friend of Sarah's. . .

"I can see you lurking, Molly," her dad said, chuckling.

Sarah smiled down at her. "I don't mind Molly staying. She's so good with the cats anyway. Last time I brought Freckles here, she was hanging on to the basket with every claw until Molly coaxed her out."

"So, who do we have here?" Sam asked, trying to look inside the basket. Sparkle had hunched himself up at the back, knowing that something was about to happen.

"It's a new kitten, Dad!" Molly told him excitedly.

"Oh, so that's why you were so keen to stay! Wow, another one, Sarah?"

Sarah shook her head. "Yes and no. I was telling Molly, he's a stray." She opened the basket, and reached in, pulling out a scrabbling Sparkle. "Hey, hey, it's all right, little one."

Molly and her dad gazed at him, almost in a trance. He was so handsome!

"I would love to keep him – but Freckle is threatening to leave home, and Maisy and Mickey keep hiding in the

kitchen cupboards." Sarah sighed sadly.

"They don't want a new kitten in their house?" Molly asked, not really surprised.

"It isn't just that. Sparkle looks sweet, but he's a bit of a nightmare. He just seems — well, odd, I suppose." Sarah looked down at Sparkle, who was now sitting on the examining table, chewing on Sam's sleeve. "He doesn't seem to like sitting still, and he's the most accident-prone cat I've ever met! He's broken two vases, and the glass in the back door. And we've only had him three days!"

Molly and her dad gave Sparkle a surprised look. That was a lot of mess for one very small kitten.

"And he's shredded half the accounts for the flower shop. I don't even know how he did it, it was in tiny little bits all over the kitchen floor. I don't know, he just seems to have to *look* at something, and it breaks. . ." She looked hopefully at Molly's dad. "I don't suppose you know anyone who wants a kitten, do you?"

"A kitten *and* a built-in paper shredder? Hmm. I'll ask around." He tickled Sparkle under the chin. "He doesn't look troublesome. Is there anything you're worried about, or do you just want him checked over?"

There was a knock on the door just then, and one of the veterinary nurses popped her head round. "Molly, your mum just called me – were you supposed to be on your way home, by any chance?" She was grinning. It was a message she had to pass on most days!

Molly gave Sparkle a longing look, and sighed. "Sorry, Jenny, I'll come now. I totally forgot. I told Mum I was only popping in to say hello. See you later, Dad! Bye Sarah, bye Sparkle."

Sparkle gazed after her as she dashed to the door, and mewed again, sadly.

Sarah smiled. "Animals just love Molly, don't they?" she said to Molly's dad.

Sam Smith nodded. "I know. I wouldn't be surprised if she became a vet when

she's older. Molly would be a fantastic vet.
She's got a magic touch."

Sparkle was
still staring
at the slowly
closing door,
but as Sam
said that he
turned to look
thoughtfully
up at him. It
was almost as if
he thought so
too. . .

Chapter Two

Sparkle's Secret

Molly thought about Sparkle lots that week. She really wanted to know how he was getting on at Sarah's and whether the other cats were starting to like him. Her dad had put up a notice in the surgery, telling people that Sparkle had been found, and did anyone know who he belonged to. Sarah had said she was going to put up some more round the town too.

"He didn't have a collar on, though,"

Molly's dad explained at breakfast on Friday. "I've a feeling we'll need to find a new home for him, if Sarah can't keep him."

Molly drifted into a daydream, imagining Sparkle's new home – with her. Sparkle sleeping curled up on her bed. Sparkle waiting to play with her when she came home from school. Sparkle sitting on her desk while she did her homework.

"No, Molly." Her mum's voice was firm, and Molly stared at her.

"What?" she asked, trying to look as though she hadn't been thinking about kittens at all.

15

"No, you are not having a cat. You're not old enough for your own pet yet. Your dad and I have seen too many animals who don't get properly looked after. You just need to be a bit older, that's all." Her mum smiled sympathetically. "Kitty's still very young for a pet, too. She'd be dressing a kitten in her doll's clothes!"

"And even if you were both old enough, from what Sarah said, I don't think I want that kitten in the house." Molly's dad shuddered.

Molly stared down at her toast, her eyes suddenly filling with tears. Poor little Sparkle. What if nobody wanted him?

Molly's grandad picked her up from school that afternoon with Kitty. He quite often did, when he wasn't working. He was the local blacksmith, and Molly loved to help him by holding the horses and ponies as he fitted their shoes.

"Grandad, can we walk home along the lane?" Molly asked hopefully. "It's a really nice day, and it hasn't rained for ages so it won't be muddy."

Kitty jumped up and down, swinging from Grandad's hand. "Yes, yes! We can look for rabbits!" Kitty and Molly had once seen wild rabbits when they were walking down the lane in the early evening, and now Kitty watched for them every time.

"Sounds good to me. Here, Molly, give me that painting, you can't carry all of that." Molly had lots of bits that she'd gathered at school during the week, and she gratefully handed her painting over.

"That's a lovely cat, Molly. Is he one you saw at the surgery?" Grandad held the painting out to admire. Molly had drawn Sparkle as she remembered him, sitting on the surgery table, watching her sadly as she had to run back to the house.

She couldn't get his little face out of her mind somehow, which was odd, as she saw so many gorgeous pets at the surgery. Sparkle just seemed extra-special. She could imagine how he was feeling, back at Sarah's cottage, trying to fit in with the other cats, lonely and wishing for a home where someone really wanted him. . . It was almost as though she could hear him asking her to help.

"Yes, that's Sparkle. He's living with Sarah. We might see him if we go home past her cottage," Molly explained hopefully.

"I might have known it would be something to do with an animal," Grandad said, grinning. "Come on then. Cats and rabbits, let's see what we can find."

Molly and Kitty raced ahead as they came near to Sarah's cottage. They hadn't seen any rabbits by the little wood, but

Grandad had promised to take Kitty out on a special rabbit-watching trip one day soon, just before bedtime.

"I can see him!" Molly called back eagerly, her school bag bumping against her legs as she skidded to a halt. "Careful, Kitty, we might scare him if we run up too fast."

"Where is he? I want to see!" Kitty pulled against Molly's arm.

"Ssshhh, ssshhh, over there, look, on the fence." Molly pointed.

Sparkle was sitting on Sarah's front fence, perfectly posed on one of the fence posts, with his tail wrapped round his paws. He was staring interestedly up the lane towards them, his ears pricked forward, and his back a little stiff, in that way that cats look when they've just seen something important − like a mouse, or a butterfly to chase.

As Molly and
Kitty walked slowly
closer, Sparkle came
to meet them,
walking along the
top of the fence
like a tightrope
walker. He ducked
his head for them
to stroke his ears,
and purred loudly. Molly could feel how
glad he was to see her.

"I wanted to see you too," she whispered
happily, watching as Kitty gently tickled
Sparkle under his chin.

Then all of a sudden Sparkle tensed
up, pulling away from Kitty, and Molly
realized that Sarah's big black-and-white
cat Mickey had just popped through the

cat flap – Mickey was so big that he had to push himself through the hole and he really did seem to pop out. Mickey stopped short as soon as he saw Sparkle, and then he hissed, and the two cats glared at each other.

"What are they doing, Molly?" Kitty asked nervously.

"I don't think Mickey likes Sparkle very much," Molly explained. "Because Sparkle's living in his house, I suppose." Hopefully Molly leaned over the fence to try and distract the big tomcat. "Mickey! Puss–puss–puss! Come and see me!"

But for once Mickey ignored her. He stalked furiously across the garden and stopped by the fence, hissing loudly at Sparkle, his tail flicking back and forth.

Sparkle hissed back, but he was standing nervously on the fence now.

Mickey prowled backwards and forwards underneath him, his tail fluffing up to twice its normal size.

"Maybe we should tell Sarah," Molly muttered worriedly. "I don't want them to fight!"

But just then Sparkle gave up. He scooted along the fence and dashed up into the safety of the big apple tree. From up there he felt brave enough to hiss and spit back at Mickey.

Molly couldn't help giggling. Now she wasn't worried about the cats hurting each other, it was quite funny watching them – she could almost imagine the rude names Sparkle was shouting at Mickey!

Sarah came round the side of the cottage carrying a basket of gardening things. "Stop it, you two!" Sarah said crossly. "Oh, hello girls, hello Ted."

"We were just about to come and tell you," Molly said. "We weren't sure if they were going to have a fight."

Mickey gave Sparkle one last furious look and stomped grumpily back over to the cat flap, squeezing himself back in. Sparkle sat on his branch, grumbling to himself, and licking his paws indignantly. He clearly wasn't at all grateful to Sarah for interrupting.

"To be honest, Molly," Sarah sighed, "I don't know what to do with them. I'm beginning to think I'm going to have to take Sparkle to the animal shelter. Him being here just isn't working. But it's so sad – he'll hate it there, shut in a tiny run. He's such a stubborn little cat, and he likes his own way."

"No one else wants him?" Molly asked miserably. Oh, if only Mum and Dad would let her have Sparkle!

Sarah shook her head. "No one that I can find."

Sparkle finished licking his paws, and

gave himself a little shake. Clearly he felt back to normal now. He stood up, and picked his way delicately along the branch to Molly. He gazed down at her, his huge green eyes glinting with excitement.

Molly laughed, rather sadly. "I can see why you call him Sparkle," she told Sarah. "His eyes really do."

Sarah seemed surprised. She looked down at Sparkle, with an odd expression on her face. "Do you know, Molly, I hadn't even thought about it before. . ." She frowned to herself. "I didn't name him Sparkle. I'm sure I didn't. It was just − his name. But he hadn't a collar, so how did I know?"

Sparkle jumped down on to the fence, and trotted back to Molly and Kitty. He stretched out his head to Molly, offering her his ears to scratch. She rubbed his soft, silky fur, and he let out a deep, rumbling purr of delight. Then he half stood on his hind paws, obviously wanting her to pick him up for a cuddle.

Molly let him jump into her arms, amazed at how light he was. She held him against her shoulder, his green eyes gazing into her blue ones, and wished and wished he was hers.

It was as though a river rushed through her mind all at once. Glittering images seemed to burst in on her, and such feelings! New things and loneliness and a desperate wish to go home. She saw huge trees, and an old lady who had lots of delicious food, and butterflies that were such fun to chase. . . *Please take me home!*

Molly jumped, dropping Sparkle, who sprang out of her arms, and leaped back to the fence. Molly stared at him in amazement, cradling her hand, and he stared back.

If cats could smile, Sparkle was smiling now. A loving, anxious, hopeful smile that was so clearly asking her for something. Had he *really* just spoken to her? She was sure he had asked her to take him home. It was strange, and a little scary, but Molly still couldn't help bubbling with wonder and happiness. She'd always dreamed of being able to talk to the animals she loved so much. Was it actually happening? Or had she just imagined it?

"Oh, Molly, I'm so sorry, did he bite you?" Sarah asked anxiously, looking at her hand.

"N-no." Molly murmured. She couldn't say what had happened. She didn't *know*. And if she said that Sparkle had *talked* to her, and that he'd felt as if he were made of glitter, and gold, and shining light, they would all think she was being silly.

Instead she just stared at the little grey cat, wondering what he'd done to her – and what he *was*.

And what she was supposed to do about it.

Chapter Three

A Midnight Visitor

Molly was silent all the way home. It was half because she couldn't believe what had just happened, and half because she was so upset that Sparkle might have to go to an animal shelter. It was lucky that Grandad explained to Mum, because Molly couldn't have told her about it without crying. If only they could find his real owner! Sarah loved cats, and if even she couldn't face keeping him, he'd never have a home. He might be at the animal shelter for ever.

He wants to go home, Molly thought miserably. *I know cats can't talk, but I'm sure he asked me to take him home!* Molly had never felt anything like the pictures and thoughts that had rushed through her when she was holding the little grey kitten. Strangely enough, that amazing stream of thoughts had felt almost *sparkly*.

Maybe that's what he was named for, Molly wondered, gazing at her fish fingers without really seeing them. *Not his sparkling green eyes at all.* Then she remembered what Sarah had said about Sparkle's name. That was *really* weird. How could a cat tell someone their name? And how had she known what Sparkle wanted, if he hadn't told her?

It sounded almost like magic. . .

★

Molly was dreaming about having her own kitten – a green-eyed grey kitten who looked just like Sparkle. He was curled up on her lap, purring deeply as she stroked him. Molly smiled in her sleep, her fingers twitching. Then her dream-kitten stood up on her lap, his ears pricked, and mewed excitedly. He turned and put his paws up on her chest, padding at her with his paws, mewing again, trying to tell her something.

Molly rolled over in bed, muttering worriedly to herself. Then she sat up suddenly. This wasn't a dream. That really was mewing! Sad, weary mewing from outside her bedroom window.

Molly blinked, and pinched herself to check that this wasn't just a very odd dream. Ow! No, she was definitely

awake. The night-light from the landing was shining into her room, but it was still half-dark, the room full of scary shadows. It must be the middle of the night.

Why would I dream about a black kitten, and then hear one mewing outside my window? Molly thought to herself. It had to be Sparkle, it just had to. He had been sending her a dream-message! Still, it was difficult to make herself get out of bed. It was so dark!

She pushed back her duvet and walked slowly over to the window, her heart thudding hard with excitement and fear. She grabbed her bedroom curtains, and took a deep breath, then pulled them open quickly.

Even though she'd been almost sure that Sparkle would be there, she still jumped back when he pressed his nose against the dark window and meowed loudly. Sparkle stood up with his front paws on the window, scrabbling against the glass. "Let me in! Oh, please let me in!"

Molly just stared at him. It was obvious that that was what he meant, but he'd actually said it. Hadn't he? A cat really had spoken to her. . . Molly put her hand over her mouth to stop herself from laughing out loud in pure delight. She didn't want to explain this to her sleepy, and probably grumpy mum and dad!

Sparkle batted the window again. "It's so cold out here! Open the window, Molly, please!"

Molly unfastened the window catch — the old farmhouse had pretty, diamond-patterned windows with deep windowsills — and waved to Sparkle to scoot along so she could open the window. He hunched himself up against the wall, and then squidged himself through the window as soon as Molly creaked it open.

"It's freezing out there," Sparkle squeaked as he leaped down from the windowsill. "You sleep very soundly, don't you? I was mewing for ages, you know." He gazed up at her, his ears laid a little back. He was obviously frozen.

"Sorry," Molly whispered, staring at him as he made himself comfortable on her bed. He had fluffed up all his fur to keep himself warm, and he looked like her nana's old-fashioned powder puff.

"Come on," Sparkle said, making himself a little nest in her duvet. "Won't you cuddle me while we work out a plan? You're lovely and warm."

"A plan?" Molly repeated, as she obediently got back into bed. She pulled the duvet up round her, and sat hugging her knees and watching this strange little creature who seemed to have taken over her bedroom.

Sparkle
looked up
at her, his
huge green
eyes full of
surprise. "Well,
of course! You
are going to take me
home, aren't you?" He stared hopefully
at her, his eyes round and worried. "Oh,
please, you have to!"

Molly gaped at him. She didn't know
what to say. Then she took a deep breath.
"I do?" she asked politely.

"You're the only person who's heard
me talking, so far," Sparkle explained.
He sounded rather upset. "I've asked
everybody," he added miserably. "No one
listened."

Molly leaned forward, interested. "Nobody else can understand you?" she asked curiously. "Only me?"

"I thought Sarah *might*," Sparkle said thoughtfully. "It was as though she almost did, but then she seemed not to want to."

"Maybe it's because she's a grown-up," Molly wondered.

"Probably." Sparkle nodded. "Yes, that might be it. She's too old to believe."

"And . . . I can hear you because I believe?" Molly asked shyly.

Sparkle gave her a cat-smile, crinkling up his eyes. "I think you must be quite special. Like my owner. That's why you're the only one who can take me back to her."

Molly nodded excitedly. "Of course I will. Where does she live?"

Sparkle sighed sadly. "I don't know!" He

was obviously embarrassed. He hunched up his shoulders, and then started to lick his paw very quickly so as not to have to look at Molly. "If I knew — I could — go back — by myself, couldn't I?" he said, his voice rather muffled by the paw-licking.

"Oh. . ." Molly said doubtfully. "But . . . I don't know where you live, either. . . Don't you have *any* idea? Is it far away?"

"Oh no, not very." Sparkle sat up eagerly. He climbed up the duvet towards Molly and started to explain. "You see, I was exploring. I *am* allowed, you know. But I'm not supposed to go out of the clearing. . ." He sighed, and his whiskers drooped.

"But you did?" Molly asked gently, stroking behind his ears.

Sparkle purred, twisting his head against her fingers. "Yes," he admitted. "Not very far, though. I was chasing a butterfly. The biggest one I've ever seen!" His eyes sparkled brightly. "I almost caught it, too. Then it fluttered off between the trees, and I'd so nearly got it, I thought it wouldn't matter. I only followed it a *little* way, really." His voice was sad suddenly, and he pulled himself away and turned his back on Molly, sitting very still. He muttered the rest. "Then it disappeared, which wasn't fair, and when I looked round to go back, I couldn't quite see which trees I was meant to go past. That butterfly cheated."

Molly couldn't help smiling. He sounded

just like Kitty. It made her see how young Sparkle was – even though he could talk, he was still only a very little cat.

"Don't worry, Sparkle. I'll get you home, I know you live by trees now," she told him encouragingly. "Are there any other clues you can tell me? What does your owner's house look like? Oh, and what's her name? I might know her, I know lots of people in Larkhill, because so many of them come to our vet's surgery."

Sparkle turned round and looked at her hopefully, but then he shook his head. "I don't think you'll know her. She doesn't often come into the town. She likes to be quiet and peaceful, and she says people are too noisy. But she doesn't mind me," he said proudly. "She's teaching me lots of things. Only I forgot about not going too far, and that's the most important thing of all." He sighed. "I probably won't get a chocolate mouse after tea."

"What about her house, then?" Molly asked, grinning to herself. He was so sweet!

Sparkle blinked. He was obviously still thinking about chocolate mice. "It's a small house. But it's lovely and cosy. My owner calls it a cottage," he said thoughtfully. "And there are lots of trees, like I said before. . . Oh, and there's a stream! I went across that after the butterfly."

Molly stared at him. She had a horrible feeling all of a sudden. "Sparkle, did you go past a big tree, one that had fallen over and had moss and toadstools growing all over it?"

"Oh yes!" Sparkle agreed happily. "I
forgot! Well done, Molly! You know
where my home is, don't you? Can you
take me back? Please?"

Molly stared at him silently, her eyes
wide with panic. He was so little, and he
was trusting her to take him home. And
the awful thing was, she *did* know where
he meant.

In the clearing, past the old hollow
tree, across the stream, deep in the middle
of Larkhill Wood.

Where the witch lived. . .

Chapter Four

The Magic Glitter

Of course, she should have known. *Who else but a witch would have a kitten who talked*, Molly thought to herself, as she watched Sparkle sleeping, stretched out on her pillow. He was snoozing blissfully,

his paws curling and uncurling as he dreamed – probably he was thinking of chocolate mice again, or scampering after those butterflies. He was so sure Molly could take him home. She couldn't let him down. But it was Larkfield Wood!

Everyone in the town knew that the middle of the wood was special, and secret, and haunted. Everyone at school said so. None of Molly's friends had ever been to the middle of the wood.

Last summer she and two of her friends from school, Kieran and Lucy, had gone on a picnic with Lucy's mum and dad to Larkfield Wood, and they'd played hide-and-seek. Kieran had dared them to run up and touch the old hollow tree, and Molly had just about managed it. She'd brushed it with her fingertips and raced away, feeling sick with fear, and sure that something horrible was chasing her.

Lucy hadn't even touched the tree.

She'd said she didn't care if Kieran told everyone in their class she was a big fat baby, *she wasn't going near that tree for anyone*. And when they went back to their picnic spot, and told Lucy's parents what they'd been playing, Lucy's mum had shaken her head, and shuddered.

"I don't blame you, Lucy!" she said, giving her a big hug. "I wouldn't either. This part of the wood is lovely, but no one goes too far in. Never past the old hollow tree."

"Why?" demanded Kieran. His mum and dad hadn't lived in Larkfield all that long, and so he didn't know all the stories.

"It's where the witch lives," Lucy's mum said simply. And she sounded so certain that even Kieran didn't laugh. He just looked thoughtfully back through the trees. Molly had stared down at her fingers, and then rubbed them hard on her shorts. They'd felt sticky, and dirty, even though they looked clean.

Now Sparkle wanted her to go even further into the wood, and over the stream. He needed Molly to find a witch's cottage – and a witch!

I suppose I could just leave him by the hollow tree, Molly thought. *But then he might not be able to find his way, and he could be lost in the scary wood, all alone. I'd have to see him all the way home, I'd have to. . .*

Molly lay awake long into the night. She couldn't let Sparkle be taken off to an animal shelter, he would hate it so much, but no one else wanted him. And anyway, Sparkle didn't want a new owner, he wanted to go home.

It wasn't just going all the way into the wood that was the only problem, Molly thought, wriggling round in bed for the thousandth time. How was she going to get Mum to let her disappear off to the woods on a secret journey? It was Saturday tomorrow, so at least she didn't have school, but she wasn't allowed out by herself except in their garden and the field. Mum would never let her go to the woods on her own.

Molly sighed, and tucked a fold of the duvet over Sparkle, in case Mum or Kitty came in early in the morning and spotted him.

When she fell asleep at last, Molly kept dreaming about enormous trees that walked, and tapped her shoulders with their long, scratchy branches. It was horrible, and she was very glad to wake up, and see the sunshine pouring through the curtains she'd left open last night. Somehow the thought of the wood wasn't quite so scary in the daylight. But there was still Mum and Dad to worry about.

Molly stared down at Sparkle, and as she watched, he opened one green eye and stared back. Then he yawned hugely, showing his tiny pointy white teeth.

"Hello," he said sleepily. Then he sat up and peered into her eyes. "What's the matter?" he asked, his ears laying back against his head. "You look worried."

Molly sighed. "I'm so sorry, Sparkle, but I don't know how I'm going to manage to take you back home. I can't exactly tell my mum I'm going off to the woods because a kitten told me to, can I?"

Sparkle nodded, and licked a paw, in a considering sort of way. "Can't you just tell her you're going for a walk?"

Molly shook her head. "No. They wouldn't let me go on my own."

Sparkle nodded. "Oh. No, I see. Like I'm not supposed to." He stared sadly at the pattern on the duvet. Suddenly he sat up straight, looking excited. "I know! We'll do a spell."

"Can you do spells?" Molly asked doubtfully.

"Oh yes! I've done lots. Well, some. If

you help, I'm sure we can do it. Do you have anything glittery?"

Molly looked round her room. "Like a necklace?"

"No, no, no! I need magic dust, and I shouldn't think you have any of that, so we have to make some." Sparkle leaped off the bed, and started to prowl around the room, sniffing hopefully.

Molly climbed out of bed and followed him. "Look, what about this?" She showed him the special art set that her nana had sent her, which had six different colours of glitter in little tubes. It was her favourite thing.

"Perfect!" Sparkle's whiskers twitched delightedly as Molly held the open tube of pink glitter under his nose. "But not so close, or I'll sneeze," he added practically.

"What will happen when we use the magic dust?" Molly asked breathlessly, her heart thumping with excitement.

Sparkle looked as though he hadn't planned that far. "Um. I'm not sure." He wrinkled his nose thoughtfully. "What do we *want* to happen?"

Molly wrinkled her nose as well. "Well . . . I suppose we want my mum and dad to let us go to Larkfield Wood. But – it's not that I don't think the magic will work, Sparkle – it's just that I'm still not sure Mum will let me go off to the woods. She'd say no to that even if she was *covered* in magic glitter, I bet she would."

They looked at each worriedly. Then
Molly gave an excited squeak. "I know!
Let's ask Mum and Dad if we can *all* go
on a picnic to Larkfield Wood. And the
magic can persuade them to say yes! Then
perhaps we can find your home while
we're all in the wood."

"Yes!" Sparkle ran round Molly in
circles, so fast his fur went blurry. "That's
just right." He skidded to a stop and
jumped back on to Molly's bed. "Come
on, bring the glitter. We've got to turn it
into magic dust." He stared at the tube
of glitter in Molly's hand, his little grey
forehead wrinkling as he thought. "You
need to think about your parents for me,
Molly – this magic dust is for them, you
see. And now we blow on it! Come on!"

He blew a slow, careful breath on to
the tube of glitter, and Molly blew too,

very softly and gently. She was trying to hold a picture of her mum and dad in her mind at the same time, and it was tricky. But to her amazement the glitter swirled up and out of the tube, spiralling round and round, sparkling and twinkling.

It whirled round Molly, wrapping her in a shimmery pink cocoon that smelled like strawberries, before it all whooshed back into its little tube again. The fiddly little stopper flew back into the tube with a pop.

Molly giggled. "That was magic! I can't believe we just did magic in my bedroom!"

Sparkle purred proudly. "I *am* clever," he admitted, ducking his head as though he was a little bit shy. "Now all we have to do is sprinkle the glitter around your parents, and Kitty." Sparkle nodded to himself, clearly pleased with their work. "Now can I have some breakfast, please? Doing magic makes me very hungry."

Molly crept downstairs and found him some tuna fish that her mum had left in the fridge from making her a packed lunch the other day. Sparkle sniffed it doubtfully, but then wolfed it down. "Is there any more?" he asked hopefully.

Molly shook her head. "No, and we haven't got any cat food. Sssshh! I can hear someone. Hide!" She looked round in a panic for somewhere to hide a little grey kitten, but Sparkle just gave her a mischievous look, and vanished.

Molly gasped with shock, then giggled as she realized what he'd done. He was so clever – and so naughty!

"I'll be back soon!" A whispery little voice seemed to float on the air. "After you've all had breakfast, use the magic glitter, and we'll be off!"

Chapter Five

Larkfield Wood

It was a beautiful day. Even though it was late September, the sun was warm, and the trees were just starting to show yellow and orange leaves amongst the green. The spell was working beautifully. They were very close to the old hollow tree. Molly tried hard to feel more pleased. . .

"This was a very good idea, Molly," Mum said, starting to unpack their picnic. "A lovely way to spend a Saturday."

Molly smiled. She looked over her

shoulder, peering into her backpack. Mum and Dad thought it was full of her rain jacket and a sun hat — Mum liked to be prepared, whatever the weather. She had just about got the sun hat in, but peeping out from underneath it was Sparkle. She could see his green eyes glittering with excitement.

"We're close!" he whispered. "I can feel it, Molly! I'm nearly home!"

Kitty was jumping about cheerfully. "Let's go and explore!" she cried. "Can we look for rabbits? I bet rabbits live here!"

"Let's have lunch first," Dad said. "I need a rest after that long walk. Come and sit down, girls."

Molly looked doubtfully at her backpack. She wasn't sure Sparkle could manage to stay still for much longer. The backpack had already done a lot of wriggling while they were walking. She sat down, making sure it was behind her, and none of the others could see it.

"Ham sandwich, Molly?" Mum held one out.

"Ahem!" A kitten cough sounded behind her, and Molly grinned. She broke off a big corner, and carefully dropped it by the backpack, while she pretended to look for her sunglasses.

Sparkle had two sandwiches and a sausage roll, and he argued for Molly's chocolate biscuit too, but Molly was sure biscuits weren't good for cats.

"Goodness, Molly, you are hungry today!" Mum commented. "It must have been the long walk."

Molly nodded, trying not to smile. While Mum and Dad packed away the rubbish, she peeped round at her backpack. Sparkle was awfully quiet.

Sparkle had gone!

Molly gasped, and grabbed the bag, hoping that she was just being stupid and he was there after all.

"Are you all right, Molly?" Dad asked, looking up.

"Oh! Yes, I . . . I just sat on a stone, that's all." Molly gave him a half-smile. Sparkle couldn't have just left, not without saying goodbye. And besides, he hadn't been sure where in the wood his home was. She gazed at the trees through tear-filled eyes. She couldn't believe he'd gone.

"Prrrp!" A little purring noise made her jump.

Sparkle popped his head out from behind a clump of ferns and grinned at her. "Come on!" he whispered. "Let's go and find the cottage!"

Molly was so relieved. She jumped up, almost forgetting she was on a secret mission. Then she remembered. "Mum, can I go and explore?"

Her mum looked unsure. Molly stared at her hopefully, and felt in her jeans pocket for the magic dust — they'd brought the last few sprinkles from the bottom of the tube, just in case.

"It'll be all right, if Molly's careful not to go too far," Dad said helpfully. "Make sure you stay where you can hear us if we call, won't you?"

"Oh yes!" Molly agreed, already following a little grey tail that was skipping off through the trees.

"Don't go disturbing any witches!" Dad shouted after her, laughing.

"I won't!" Molly called back, wishing over and over that that wasn't exactly what she was planning to do.

A couple of minutes later, Molly looked over her shoulder nervously. She could only just see Dad's red sweatshirt now.

She knew they weren't far at all from their picnic spot, but it felt like she and Sparkle were on their own in the wood. It was silent – just like her dream. The trees weren't actually following her, but they did have long twiggy branches, that looked as if they might reach out and catch her hair.

"What's the matter?" Sparkle asked, trotting back to her.

Molly gave up trying to pretend she wasn't scared. It wasn't working very well. "I don't like it here," she whispered. "It's spooky."

Sparkle looked around, surprised. "Is it?"

Molly rubbed her hands over her arms. She was cold, even in the warm sunlight. "Yes," she said firmly. "I know you don't think so, but it is! Oh, look, there's the hollow tree." Molly pointed, her hand shaking slightly. She could just hear Kitty laughing at something in the distance. *They aren't far!* she told herself firmly.

"Oh yes! Well done, Molly!" Sparkle ran ahead and leaped on to the tree, running up and down it in a mad kitten dance. "Is it much further from here?" he asked her hopefully, when he eventually stopped twirling around after his tail.

"I'm not sure," Molly said, taking a deep, shivery breath. "I think we just have to look. Do you remember where you were when you saw the hollow tree, on the day you got lost?"

Sparkle hopped down, and trotted over to the side of the clearing. "Maybe this way?" he said thoughtfully. "Or that way? Oooh, there are some gorgeous smells over here! It smells like mouse!" He bounded off behind a bush.

"Don't go too far!" Molly called anxiously. "Don't get lost. . ."

But then her voice trailed off.

There was someone else coming through the trees. . .

Chapter Six

Sparkle's Gift

Walking towards her was an old lady
who looked quite like her nana. She was
smiling, but she looked anxious. "You
haven't seen a kitten, have you, while you
were walking? A grey kitten, quite small.
The silly little thing went off exploring, a
few days ago." She sighed. "I'm sure he's
safe, I'd know if he wasn't, but I do wish
I knew where he'd got to."

Molly gulped, and said very quietly and
very fast, "He's-over-there!" Then she shut

her mouth with a snap. She didn't think it was a good idea to talk to witches. Not without being asked, anyway.

The old lady looked at her closely. "What did you say, dear? Are you all right?"

Molly nodded. She was still too nervous

to say anything, but the witch didn't seem as frightening as she had expected. She wasn't even wearing black.

Suddenly the old lady gasped. "Sparkle! Oh, you're back, you silly kitten, where have you been?" And she crouched down, reaching out to Sparkle, who was racing across the clearing towards them. He was so excited that he was leaving a trail of tiny pink and golden stars floating behind him as his paws touched the grass, and he flung himself into the old lady's arms, purring with delight.

Molly laughed, his happiness was so catching, but she couldn't help feeling the tiniest bit sad. She wouldn't see Sparkle again now. It had been so lovely to imagine him being hers, but now she knew it was never going to happen. She gave a little sigh, and realized that Sparkle was telling the old lady about his adventures.

"And Molly had some pink glitter, and I put a spell on it, so she could bring me home!" he finished triumphantly.

The witch looked a little bewildered, but she smiled gratefully at Molly. "Thank you so much, Molly dear. It was very brave of you to come, and very clever to think of bringing everyone on a picnic. I can't think that you wanted to come deeper into the wood, did you?"

Molly smiled shyly and shook her head.

"She was scared," Sparkle said. "*I* wasn't." He jumped down and started to bat at grass seeds with his tiny paws.

The witch gave Molly an apologetic look. "Kittens can be very rude sometimes," she said, smiling. "Won't you come and tell me how you found Sparkle? Let's sit on the old tree for a bit, my legs aren't what they used to be."

Molly looked at the tree. Somehow it didn't seem scary any more. It had dark green velvety moss that looked just like cushions. She sat down next to the old lady, and they watched Sparkle stalking an imaginary mouse.

"Can you speak to all animals?" the witch asked Molly curiously.

Molly stared back at her. "I don't think so," she said in surprise. "Sparkle is the only one who's ever spoken to *me*. Do you think I might meet more animals who talk?" she asked hopefully. She explained about living at the vet's.

The witch nodded slowly. "I think you've been given a very special gift. It must be for a reason."

Molly stared worriedly back at her. That sounded a bit scary. "You mean, I have to go on a – a quest, or something like that?" she asked, thinking about stories that she'd read.

"No, I think you should stay right where you are," the witch said, smiling. "Sparkle found you, didn't he, when he needed someone. You see so many animals, you'll just need to keep an eye out for the special ones. The ones who need your gift."

Molly nodded, smiling to herself. More magical animals! It was so exciting! Then she looked anxious. "But what if I can't help? I only managed to bring Sparkle home because I knew where you lived. And I almost didn't help, even then," she added very quietly, feeling rather ashamed of herself.

"But you *did*, Molly. That's what matters. It wouldn't have been brave if Sparkle had just lived down the street, would it?" The witch stared thoughtfully into the distance, and then reached a hand into the air. When she brought it down again, something glittery was dangling from it. She passed it to Molly, who was watching wide-eyed. "For you, to say thank you."

Sparkle ran back and jumped on to Molly's lap to see what it was. "Oh!

Pretty!" he said, patting at it with a paw. It was a silver chain with a little stone pendant dangling from it, in the shape of a cat's head.

"It's beautiful," Molly breathed, holding it in her hand.

"It opens, do you see?" the witch explained, pointing out a tiny catch at the side. She took a tiny pair of golden scissors from her pocket. "You can put something inside."

She beckoned to Sparkle, and whispered in his ear. He twitched his tail reluctantly. "*Must* I?" he whined. "If you cut one off, they won't match. Oh, I suppose so!" He pointed his nose towards her, sighing heavily, and she snipped off one of his whiskers.

"Now, put it inside the locket," the witch explained, dropping the shining whisker into Molly's hand. It sparkled a little as she folded it round into the tiny space. "If you ever need our help, you can call us with it, you see."

"It's very special, you know, one of my whiskers. Thank you, Molly, for bringing me home." Sparkle put his paws on Molly's arm, and reached up to touch her nose with his. A kitten kiss. Molly smiled down at him, feeling the glittery magic as his whiskers brushed her cheek.

Somewhere a bird called, breaking the spell, and Molly gasped. "Oh! What time is it?" she asked, jumping down from the tree. "We've been away ages, haven't we?" It felt as though she and Sparkle had been in that strange, magical wood for hours.

The witch smiled. "They won't have missed you. It's really only been a few minutes."

Molly nodded slowly. Had it only been that long? It felt as if her whole life had changed, in just a moment. She leaned over to hug Sparkle one last time, and he purred gratefully in her ear.

"Goodbye!" Molly called, and she ran on a few steps, anxious to get back, and see whether her parents really hadn't worried about her. She turned to wave one last time, to say thank you for her beautiful present.

But they were gone. There was no old lady sitting on the hollow tree, no sparkling grey cat.

Molly stared through the trees, a little doubtfully, and then her hand closed tightly around the cat locket. "Goodbye!" she whispered, smiling, sure they could hear her. Then she ran on into the clearing where she could see Kitty and her parents waving. Molly waved back excitedly.

She was already wondering what her next adventure would be.

Turn over for an extract from Holly
Webb's brand new series about Sophie
and her super squeaky and furry friends!

CHAPTER ONE

Sophie peered out over the view, watching the sunlight sparkle on the windows, and wondering who lived there, under the roofs. She couldn't see her own house from here, or she didn't think she could, anyway. She hadn't lived in Paris for long enough to know.

The city *was* very beautiful, but it still didn't feel like home. Sophie sighed, and rested her chin on her hands. She missed her old house, and her old bedroom, and her cat, Oscar. Grandma was looking after him while they lived in Paris, but Sophie was sure that Oscar missed her, almost as much as she missed him.

"What are you looking at?" Dan squashed up next to her, leaning over the stone balcony.

"Just things," Sophie said vaguely. "The view."

"Boring," Dan muttered. "This is taking ages. And I'm hungry." He turned round, holding his tummy in both hands and made a starving face at Sophie. His nose scrunched up like a rabbit's, and Sophie smirked. She crossed her eyes and poked her tongue out at the corner of her mouth to make Dan laugh. After all, even a wonderful view can be boring when you've been looking at it for a *VERY LONG TIME.*

All the people who live in Paris love their city so much, and many of them walk up the steep steps to the church on their wedding days to have their photographs taken next to the wonderful view. But it can take an awful long time to get the photographs right, especially when it's windy and your auntie's wedding dress won't stay still properly.

"Sophie and Dan! Stop making faces like that! You're making Dad giggle, and he's supposed to be taking romantic photos!" Mum glared at them, but Dad rolled his eyes, and stuck his tongue out at Dan. Sophie thought Dad might be a bit bored with the photos as well.

This church was one of Sophie's favourite places in Paris. It was so pretty, and there was the fountain to look at, and all the people. She even liked its name, *Sacré Coeur*, which meant Sacred Heart. Sophie thought it was very special to have a whole church that was all about love. Auntie Lou's wedding had been beautiful too, but Sophie had got up early for Mum to curl her hair and fuss over her dress, and she was tired of having to stand still and smile.

"Go and play," Auntie Lou suggested.

"Go and run around for a bit. You can come back and be in the photos later."

"Later?" Dad moaned. "I thought we'd nearly finished!" But Sophie and Dan were already halfway down the white marble steps, and couldn't hear him.

"I wish we'd brought a ball..." Dan said, as they stopped in front of the fountain that stood below the balcony. He was looking at the grassy slope of the hill. "Do you think Mum would mind if we went home and got one? It wouldn't take five minutes."

"Yes, she would! And anyway, even *you* couldn't play football on that grass," Sophie pointed out. "It would just roll down to the bottom."

"Exactly. That would make it more fun! Uphill football, I've just invented it. I might be famous!"

Sophie shook her head. "I don't think all the people taking photos would be very impressed either. There are loads of them. They'd tell you off."

"Huh." But Dan looked round at all the visitors, and realized Sophie was right. No one looked as if they wanted to play football. And there was an old lady sitting on the bench over there with a really pointy umbrella, the kind with a parrot's head handle. She looked like she'd happily use the pointy end to stab footballs, and even the parrot seemed to be giving him a fierce glare.

"Race you up and down the balustrades then!" He grabbed her hand and hurried her down the two flights of stairs to the path.

Sophie squirmed. The balustrades were the stone slopes at the sides of the steps. They were wide and flat, and Dan loved to run up and down them. He'd discovered the game the first time they came to visit the church, just after they'd moved to Paris, and since *Sacré Coeur* was on their way home from school, he'd been practising. But the game made Sophie feel sick, especially when it had been raining and the stone was all slick and slippery. She was sure that he would fall off.

"Come on, Sophie!" Dan hopped up to the stonework. "You get up on the other side. Bet I can beat you back to the top!"

Sophie stood on the bottom step, looking anxiously at the flat white slope. She didn't want to run up it — but if she refused, Dan would keep on and on teasing her.

"Baby!" her brother called scornfully, and Sophie scowled. She was only a year younger than Dan! She was not a baby! Carefully, the tip of her tongue sticking out between her teeth, she stepped on to the balustrade. It wasn't really so very high, after all... And Dan looked so surprised that she'd done it! Sophie grinned at him.

"Go!" Dan yelled, dashing away up the slope. Sophie gasped, and raced after him,

wishing she had trainers on, and not her
best shoes with the glittery bows.

She slithered a little, and gasped and
reached out her hands to balance,
wishing there was something to hold on
to – a tree maybe. But there was only
the perfect short green grass, and every

so often those funny little cone-shaped bushes that almost looked like upside-down ice creams.

Halfway to the top, Dan let out a yell as he spotted one of his friends from school on the other side of the hill. He hopped down and raced across the grass to see Benjamin, leaving Sophie glaring after him. He'd just abandoned their race, after she'd been brave enough to climb the balustrade at last. How could he? She folded her arms and tapped her foot crossly on the stone. Brothers! They were so rude!

If only she had a friend to play with, too. It wasn't fair. Sophie watched Dan and Benjamin chasing each other across the grass, and sighed sadly. Somehow, she just hadn't found anybody she liked that much at school yet. Even though Mum had spoken French to them ever since they were little, Sophie still felt as though she wasn't doing it quite right. The teachers told her she was doing ever so well, but the girls in her class looked at her funny whenever she opened her mouth. And then they just ran off. After some days at school, Sophie wondered if she might forget how to talk at all. It was nothing like back home. Mum had suggested sending emails to her friends from their school in London, and Sophie had, but it wasn't the same at all. All the fun things that Elizabeth and Zara told her in their replies only made Sophie feel more left out.

The only girls who'd really spoken to her were Chloe and Adrienne, and that was because their teacher had asked them to look after the new girl. Sophie had decided halfway through the first morning that she'd much rather be unlooked-after. Chloe didn't do anything except twitch her nose and giggle, which was boring, though bearable, but Sophie thought

Adrienne was possibly the nastiest person she had ever met. Because her voice was so sweet and soft, the things she said sounded perfectly nice at first. It was only when Sophie thought back that she realized how horrible they actually were.

"So, why *did* you move here?" Adrienne had a way of looking at Sophie with her head on one side that made Sophie feel like she was some ugly sort of beetle.

"Your French is quite good. For an English person, I mean..."

"I suppose that's an *English* skirt. It's very ... interesting."

Sophie gave a little shiver, even though the sun was warm on her bare shoulders. It was a hot September afternoon, but Adrienne's pretty voice was like cold water trickling down her spine, even when she was only remembering it.

She sighed again, and then shuddered as Dan and Benjamin started a race, rolling down the grassy slope.

And then she fell off.

Afterwards, Sophie wasn't quite sure how she did it. She hadn't even been moving. But her feet seemed to slip suddenly from underneath her, and then her arms were flapping uselessly at the air. There was a thump, and she was flat

on the grass on her tummy, next to one
of those strange little cone-shaped bushes.

Sophie lay there, gasping and trying
not to cry. She wanted Dan to come and
pick her up – but at the same time she
didn't want him knowing she'd been silly
enough to fall.

"Are you all right?"

It wasn't Dan. The mystery voice was
speaking in French, and Dan would have
spoken to her in English. It just didn't
sound like Dan, anyway. Sophie hoped
it wasn't the old lady with the parrot
umbrella. She would probably say it
was all Sophie's own fault, and insist on
taking her back to Mum and Dad and

Auntie Lou and the endless photographs.

But surely even a very little old lady wouldn't have such a high, squeaky voice?

Sophie turned her head slightly, and squeaked herself.

Staring at her worriedly was a tiny furry face, ginger-and-white, with neat little ears, and shining eyes.

"Are you hurt?" the squeaky voice said again, and this time there was no doubt about it. It was definitely this small furry person who was talking to her.

"No, I'm not. Thank you for asking,"

Sophie whispered, trying to sit up.

"Oh, good. Yes, that's right. Much better." The guinea pig – for now that she was the right way up, Sophie could see that's what the furry little person was – nodded approvingly. "You didn't hit your head?"

"I don't think so," Sophie murmured, shaking it gently. Though if she had bumped her head, it would explain why she was talking to a guinea pig. And, more importantly, how the guinea pig seemed to be talking back.

"Are you imaginary?" she asked, wondering if she had actually hit her head *very hard.*

"Certainly not!" The guinea pig's voice became even squeakier. Sophie was surprised it could manage it. "Whatever gave you that idea?" it asked indignantly.

"Well. You're talking. And ... and you've got a pink ballet skirt on."

The guinea pig looked down at her middle – now she'd noticed the skirt, Sophie was guessing that the guinea pig was probably a girl. Then she flounced the skirt with her little pink paws and did a twirl, gazing at her plump middle with a great deal of satisfaction. "I know. I found it yesterday. Do you like it? I think it suits me very well. But I suppose you haven't seen that many guinea pigs wearing clothes

before. I can see why you'd be surprised."

"Actually, my friend Elizabeth from home is always trying to dress up her hamster," Sophie admitted. "But he bites her, every time. It was really the talking that seemed so unusual."

"Oh..." The guinea pig looked faintly worried, and her tiny round ears twitched. "It's just possible that I shouldn't have spoken to you. It *is* meant to be a secret, actually. But I was frightened that you were hurt. You were lying so still. I'm sure the others will understand." She smoothed the pink net of her skirt with anxious little pats of her paws.

"I promise I won't tell anybody," Sophie said quickly. "It was very nice of you to be worried about me." Then she frowned. "But if you're supposed to be a secret, should you be standing there like that? Everyone can see you."

The guinea pig let out a panicked

breath of a squeak. "Mercy me! I haven't even got my hat on! Do excuse me a moment." She whisked round, and disappeared under the little cone-shaped bush in a blur of ginger fur and shocking-pink net.

A minute later she was back, with a neat circle of grass attached to the top of her head. It was held on with a green ribbon, tied in a large bow under her chin.

"We'll be all right now," the guinea pig told Sophie. "Thank you for noticing, I can't think how I came to be so careless. I'll forget my own name next. It's Josephine," she added. "I didn't tell

you, did I?" She
bobbed Sophie
a little curtsey,
holding out the
ballet skirt with
her paws.

Sophie looked
around nervously. She
wasn't sure that the grassy hat was
actually enough of a disguise. The
guinea pig still looked very much like
a guinea pig, except that now she had
long green tufty hair. There were people
climbing the stone steps past them all the
time. She wondered if she should offer to
let the guinea pig hide under the edge of

her skirt. "It's very nice to meet you. I'm Sophie. But. . ."

"I promise. . ." A little pink paw was resting on Sophie's lap. "No one will see. We've been here for so many years, you know. And no one ever does notice us. After all, it's such a silly story! A family of guinea pigs living underneath the beautiful church of *Sacré Coeur*? No one would ever believe it!"